COSMIC CLASH

SCRIPT WRITTEN BY JIM KRIEG
ADAPTED BY J. E. BRIGHT

SCHOLASTIC INC.

ISBN: 978-0-545-86801-3

10 9 8 7 6 5 4 3 2 1 16 17 18 19 20

Printed in the U.S.A. 40

First printing 2016

Book design by Erin McMahon

CHAPTER 1: HIDE-AND-GO-SEEK

BATMAN HEADED TO the Hall of Justice in his Batwing. *Strange to think that only last year I was hesitant to join the Justice League,* he thought. *Now I could not be more proud to be a member of the most dedicated and professional band of heroes history has ever known! Let's see what they're doing.* He turned on a screen.

The monitor showed Superman in the Hall of Justice, leaning his head against a wall with his eyes

closed. He was counting down from ten.

Behind him, The Flash zipped back and forth in the Hall, panicked.

Superman paused counting. “Flash, I can hear you trying to find a hiding spot. Better hurry!”

The Flash dashed away.

“Ready or not, here I come!” announced Superman. He immediately spotted a green, glowing, transparent armchair in the middle of the Hall.

Superman flew over. “Green Lantern is behind the armchair.”

Green Lantern glared at Superman. “No fair,” he protested. “We said no using superpowers. X-ray vision, much?”

“I didn’t,” said Superman. “It was the only piece of green furniture.”

Outside the Hall, Superman found Cyborg lying down, seemingly floating in midair. “Cyborg is in

Wonder Woman's Invisible Jet," he called.

Cyborg sat up. "Dang! How does he do it?"

"I keep telling you," replied Superman. "Wonder Woman's plane is invisible . . . except for the person in it."

"Why would that be helpful?" wondered Cyborg. As he climbed out of the Invisible Jet, he stepped on a button on the dashboard. Something beeped.

Two missiles launched from the jet, rocketing around the Hall. They locked onto Cyborg's heat signature, and rushed at him.

Wonder Woman swooped over and blocked the

missiles with her bracelets.

"I found Wonder Woman!" called Superman.

Cyborg hung his head. "Aw, I'm sorry, Wonder Woman. You gave up your hiding space and lost the game to keep me from doing something dumb. I know how competitive you are."

The Flash sped over. He wore a t-shirt with the words "I LOVE NY" printed on it. "Ha, you couldn't find me. I hid in the perfect place."

"New York?" asked Superman.

"How does he do it?" blurted The Flash.

Superman pointed at his t-shirt.

"Oh, heh," laughed The Flash. He spun into a blur and changed back into his usual costume.

"Superman, you really are the best at hide-and-go-seek," said Wonder Woman. "You can find anybody."

"Gee, thanks," said Superman. "When I was in the Scouts as a kid they always told me to be prepared . . ." He trailed off as his teammates stared behind him.

Batman cleared his throat.

"Oh, hey, Batman," said Cyborg nervously. "Uh . . . we were just . . . um, honing our skills of camouflage . . . and—"

"Being stealthy," added The Flash. "You know, like you!"

Batman narrowed his eyes. "Instead of performing your scheduled duties of monitoring the world for injustice, you were playing hide-and-go-seek."

"Gee whiz, Bruce," said Superman, "I'm sorry we didn't invite you to play—"

"Secret identities are not to be mentioned while in costume," Batman broke in, "as stated in the Justice League rule book. Page one!"

Wonder Woman smiled at Batman apologetically. "Our friendly exercise didn't seem like the kind of thing you'd enjoy. Not like . . . fighting crime."

"I understand completely," growled Batman. "My dark and mysterious nature terrifies criminals, intimidates my enemies, and discourages friendships."

"Don't be silly," said Superman. "Of course you're our friend! We're all friends. We're like . . . super friends!"

"Super best friends," said Cyborg.

"Batman—" began Superman, but a loud beeping alarm cut him off.

Cyborg's head flashed with bright red light.

CHAPTER 2: THE COLLECTOR

"IT'S CYBORG'S MOBILE TROUBLE ALERT!"
said Wonder Woman.

Out of Cyborg's robotic eye, a beam projected a hologram of the Earth in orbit.

"The threat appears to be space-based," said Batman. "Readjust the League's satellite to coordinates Delta twenty-seven, grid five."

"On it," said Cyborg. He concentrated. The hologram shifted, zooming out from Earth to show the surrounding area.

Green Lantern pointed at a weird dot in the hologram. "I see something!"

"Increasing resolution," said Cyborg.

The image focused on the dot, revealing a spaceship shaped like a squid with an angry skull.

"Oh, no," sighed Superman.

"You know what this is?" asked The Flash.

"Yes," replied Superman. "We have to stop it before it reaches Earth. To the *Javelin*!"

The Justice League hurried into their spaceship.

Batman strapped himself into the chair in the cockpit. "Prepare for launch," he announced.

"Everyone buckle in."

"Ah, who needs a seatbelt?" The Flash scoffed. "I run faster than this bucket flies—"

"Blastoff!" shouted Batman, pushing the throttle. The *Javelin* launched off the Earth.

The Flash tumbled out of his seat and smashed into the back wall.

"Everyone needs to buckle up," said Batman. "Every time."

Batman peered at the spaceship blinking on his monitor. "Superman, do you know what this thing is?"

"Unfortunately," Superman replied. "That ship belongs to a sentient robot named Brainiac."

The Flash streaked back into his seat and buckled up. He smiled at Cyborg. "More like *dumb-name-iac*. Am I right?" He held out his hand for a high five.

Cyborg groaned. "I'm high-fiving you for that, but my heart isn't in it."

"Brainiac was designed to be the ultimate artificial intelligence," said Superman. "He was built to catalog the existing universe for future generations. Due to an accident and a glitch in his programming, Brainiac now scours the galaxy looking for planets to capture and permanently preserve in his growing collection."

Wonder Woman leaned forward. "How can Brainiac capture entire civilizations?"

"One word," replied Superman. "Shrink-ray."

The *Javelin* approached Brainiac's ship. It loomed above them, with its vast metal skull staring down with angry eyes.

"All right, team," announced Batman, "this is a Class One threat, so I want you to—"

"Enough talk!" Green Lantern interrupted. "I'm not afraid of this overgrown calculator with attitude."

"Lantern, we all know you're fearless," replied Batman. "Just wait until—"

Green Lantern bolted off the *Javelin* in a burst of green light.

Batman shook his head. "At least I can make a plan for the rest of—"

The rest of the Justice League had already joined Green Lantern out in space.

As Batman followed his teammates in the *Javelin*, weapon bays opened on Brainiac's ship.

A pale green robot appeared in a huge hologram. "Please identify yourselves by name," Brainiac instructed in a mechanical voice. "I prefer to defeat you in alphabetical order."

"The Justice League will not be filed, stamped, indexed, cataloged, or collected!" Batman replied over the *Javelin*'s loudspeaker.

Brainiac frowned. "Then you will be deleted," he said. His hologram vanished as hundreds of missiles whistled out of launch bays. Blasts of searing light shot out of the front of the space torpedoes.

Wonder Woman dove in front of her teammates and blocked the beams with the golden cuffs on her wrists. "Boys," she said. "Always fighting." She called

over to Brainiac's spaceship. "Perhaps we can solve this peacefully!"

Immediately, she was bombarded with missiles.

"Hey, okay," Wonder Woman replied. "You asked for it, buddy!" With a warrior's cry, she lassoed a missile, and sent it rocketing back toward Brainiac. It exploded on his ship's skull eye.

Cyborg laughed. "You gave him a black eye!"

Brainiac projected his holographic image in space again. "Units of Earth," he announced angrily, "I have selected your planet for permanent backup in my archives. Prepare to be downsized. Activating shrink-ray." The skull's mouth opened, and a red light glowed from inside.

"I've got this," said Superman. He soared in front of the sun, then dived toward the spaceship, punching the skull on its chin.

The mouth snapped closed.

"My shrink-ray!" gasped Brainiac. "You broke it!"

"Nothing like soaking up some rays from Mr. Sunshine to charge up my powers," said Superman. He grabbed one of the humongous metal tentacles on Brainiac's ship and began whipping the vessel around him. He let go of the tentacle, and Brainiac's spaceship flung away into deep space.

"That should do it," Superman said. "Sometimes I forget how much power I absorb from the sun."

Batman watched Brainiac's ship on the *Javelin*'s scanner. "Brainiac has regained control, but is retreating."

The Justice League cheered in celebration.

CHAPTER 3: BRAINIAC COMES BACK

THE NEXT MORNING in the Hall of Justice, the teammates rehashed their victory over coffee.

"Did you see the way Superman threw that thing?" asked Cyborg. "He put some serious spin on it!"

Superman laughed. "I couldn't have done it without the help of my closest friends."

Wonder Woman, Green Lantern, Cyborg, and The Flash grinned at Superman.

Batman was alone across the Hall, busy working at a computer console.

"And also my work colleagues," Superman added.

"Don't mind Batman," said Green Lantern. "He's probably thinking up sneaky new ways to destroy you with Kryptonite or defeat the rest of us."

"Actually, Green Lantern," replied Batman, "I was thinking that we need to figure out the trajectory of Brainiac's retreat. Best to be prepared when he decides to make a return visit."

"Return?" The Flash scoffed. "After a spanking like that? I'm betting we'll never see that freak again."

The Trouble Alert beeped loudly, red lights flashing. The Justice League rushed over to Batman's monitor.

Brainiac had returned in a new, smaller spaceship.

Superman stretched out his shoulders. "Not a problem. I'll deal with it."

"Despite our quick victory last time, Brainiac is a formidable foe," warned Batman. "I think we should come up with a game plan."

"Yeah, okay," replied Superman. He thought for a moment. "Green Lantern, do you want to come, too?"

"I'm not afraid of that monotone metronome," declared Green Lantern.

"Wonder Woman?" asked Superman.

"Absolutely," said Wonder Woman.

Wonder Woman, Superman, and Green Lantern soared out of the Hall of Justice.

Cyborg and The Flash sat next to Batman in front of the monitors.

"This is going to be good," said Cyborg excitedly. "I bet Superman is really going to make this guy regret coming back."

Batman shook his head as he watched Superman, Green Lantern, and Wonder Woman approaching Brainiac's new ship in space.

"That's far enough, Brainiac!" declared Superman.

"The three most powerful units of the Justice League," replied Brainiac. "How fortuitous. My calculations indicated that you are the exact units I need to eliminate in order to acquire Planet Earth." A giant cannon stuck out of the front of his spaceship.

"That energy signature," said Batman. "A temporal anomaly! Superman, Wonder Woman, Green Lantern, get out of there!"

A stream of purple energy shot out of the cannon and zapped Green Lantern, Wonder Woman, and Superman. The heroes vanished in the blindingly brilliant ray.

"They're gone!" screeched Cyborg. "Brainiac destroyed Superman. And Wonder Woman. And Green Lantern." He fell on the ground sobbing.

"Oh, no!" cried The Flash. He zoomed around, freaking out. "I can't believe it! Brainiac won!"

"They're not gone, Flash," said Batman. "They're simply . . . lost in time. The Hall of Justice sensors picked up a temporal anomaly just before Brainiac's ray fired off. If I'm right—"

"And when is he not?" Cyborg said.

"Brainiac knows he doesn't have the firepower to destroy the League—" continued Batman.

"But he can send them back through time?" The Flash guessed.

Cyborg hopped over to the computer, quickly programming. "I can trace the residual temporal currents and calibrate a device that can pinpoint when in time they've been placed."

He decoded the three energy signatures, connecting them to dates. The computer calculated the years 10,000 BC, 1741 AD, and 2116 AD.

"There they are," said The Flash. He gasped. "Does this mean we're going to build what I think we're going to build?"

"It's only been a theory," agreed Batman. "But we have to try! Can you get us to the Batcave quickly?" he asked The Flash.

"No problem!" said The Flash. "Fast is my middle name!" He handed two strong cords to Batman and Cyborg. "Tow ropes. Hold on!" The Flash sprinted out of the Hall, dragging Batman and Cyborg behind him like superfast water skiers. They arrived at the Batcave in minutes.

"Sorry it took so long to get here," said The Flash. "Four minutes! You know what would be great? If there was a tunnel all the way from Metropolis to Gotham City."

"Yeah, I'll get right on that," growled Batman. "In the meantime, we've got a job to do."

They worked together to build a brand-new machine from Batman's plans. Cyborg used his knowledge of hi-tech to assist, while The Flash

rushed around gathering tools when needed. They completed the machine in record time. The Flash welded the big device to the back of the Batmobile.

"She's gorgeous," said Cyborg with an admiring whistle. "She's . . . what is she?"

"The Cosmic Treadmill," The Flash answered. "She's a time machine powered by my super-speed."

"At least in theory," cautioned Batman. "We've never tested it. Once activated it could create a rift in the time stream causing a chain reaction throughout the universe and all of space and time might collapse in on itself."

Cyborg's eyes widened. "That would not be good." Suddenly, his head beeped in alarm and blazed with warning lights.

"Trouble Alert!" said The Flash.

A hologram shot out of Cyborg's eye, showing Brainiac.

"Greetings, Earth units," the alien robot announced. "I am Brainiac and I bring good news."

"This is being broadcast all over the world," said Cyborg. "I've got built-in satellite, Wi-Fi, and AM/FM radio, and he's on every channel."

"Soon I will begin cataloging every species on this planet," continued Brainiac, "in order to create a precise record for posterity."

Cyborg's screen showed the streets of Metropolis, where Brainiac's drones were materializing, floating in the air. They scanned people with lasers. The citizens screamed and scattered.

"That doesn't sound so bad," said The Flash.

"Once finished," said Brainiac, "I will shrink your planet to a more efficient file size, place it inside a glass bottle, and store it safely in my library of civilizations for eternity. You're welcome."

"That part I'm not so crazy about," The Flash said.

Batman jumped into the Batmobile. "No time for a test run," he said. "We've got to retrieve Superman, Wonder Woman, and Green Lantern before Brainiac finishes indexing the planet. Flash, it's all up to you."

"What about me?" asked Cyborg.

"Return to the Hall of Justice and call in any available auxiliary leaguers," instructed Batman. "See if you can slow down Brainiac's indexing process."

A swirling vortex opened in front of the vehicle. The Batmobile hit the warp in time and vanished in a burst of brilliance.

CHAPTER 4: THE SAVAGE PAST

THE COSMIC TREADMILL carried the Batmobile through time, popping back into the world atop a prehistoric mountain, with primeval jungle all around.

Batman leaped out of the driver's seat. The Flash started to slow down.

"Stay put!" Batman warned. "You have to keep running. If you stop, the Cosmic Treadmill will snap back to our own era, trapping us here forever."

"Okay, so I guess I'll just keep running, then," The Flash replied. "And you?"

Batman rummaged in the Batmobile's trunk. "The first rule of infiltrating a different time era is camouflage. I'll need to blend in." He got dressed in animal skins and a prehistoric Utility Belt. He looked like a Batman caveman.

"You keep that in your car?" asked The Flash.

"Yes," replied Batman. He pulled a handheld computer out of his belt. The gadget pinged softly. "It looks like the reading is west of here. I'll scout it out. You keep running."

Batman followed his pinging device deep into the forest, where he found a cave entrance. He snuck into the cavern, but the sound of the ping gave him away. A brutish cavewoman caught him with a lasso.

The cavewomen tied him together with someone Batman recognized. It was Vandal Savage, a vicious, immortal criminal who he knew all too well from his own time. The prehistoric women hung them from a long rope above a pit of bubbling lava.

Surrounding the lava pit, the cavewomen thumped their spears against the ground. "Queen! Queen! Queen!" they chanted. Flanked by female guards, the queen of the cavewomen stepped out of the shadows

"Wonder Woman," breathed Batman.

"Silence, miscreant male!" yelled Wonder Woman. "You have been caught sneaking in with the evil Vandal Savage. For that, you will be cleansed in the fire of the mountain."

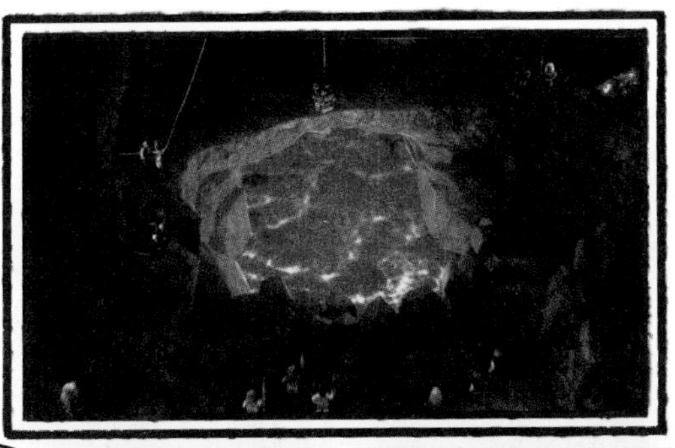

Hmmm, Batman thought. *Apparently Brainiac's Time-Beam is so jarring, it creates a form of amnesia. If I can get her to remember who she is, the time stream's natural elasticity should reject her, sending*

her back to our own time. But how . . . ?

"Lower them into the fire!" ordered Wonder Woman.

"Wonder Woman!" hollered Batman. "Wait! You don't remember me," explained Batman, "but I have come to bring you home."

"Home?" repeated Wonder Woman. "I know no home but here."

The cavewoman pointed to a cave wall, where

primitive drawings had been scratched in the rock. One illustration showed Vandal picking on the cavewomen, while the next drawing showed Wonder Woman freeing them.

"When queen arrived," a cavewoman declared, "she led glorious revolt against Vandal Savage's cavemen!"

"I am not one of them," Batman replied. "Think, Wonder Woman! You know me! I'm your . . . I'm your co-worker. I'm Batman!"

"Batman?" the cavewoman repeated with a laugh. "You think great queen would ally herself with a man?"

Batman puffed up his chest. "I, Batman, challenge the Queen of the Cavewomen to ritual trial by combat."

The prehistoric women gasped.

Batman smirked at Wonder Woman. "Or do you fear to do battle against a man?

"I fear no man!" replied Wonder Woman.

"Combat!" the cavewomen chanted.

They released Batman from the ropes that bound him to Savage. He strode to the center of the arena where Wonder Woman awaited.

"I will make this quick," declared Wonder Woman.

I only have one chance at this, thought Batman, as he and Wonder Woman circled one another in the arena. *My timing must be perfect.*

Wonder Woman charged at Batman.

Batman barreled toward her.

They leaped into the air at the same time, bellowing battle cries.

But Batman didn't try to hit her. Instead, he spun off to the side, avoiding her grasping grip. He snatched the golden lasso from her side. Batman pivoted and tossed the lasso's loop around Wonder Woman's shoulders, cinching her tight.

Wonder Woman strained against the lasso's super-strong cord. "No rope can hold me, man."

"I don't need it to hold you," replied Batman. "I need it to make you tell the truth. Who are you?" asked Batman.

"I . . . am queen of the—" stammered Wonder Woman uncertainly.

Batman gripped the golden rope tighter. "The magic lasso compels you to speak the truth. Even a truth you've forgotten."

Wonder Woman squirmed in internal struggle as the lasso brightened its golden glow.

"I *am* Wonder Woman!" she realized, flying up to hover triumphantly.

The cavewomen cheered.

Wonder Woman shook her head, clearing the last of her amnesia. "Prehistoric Persephone," she shouted in amazement. "Batman! You rescued me. But how?"

"No time to explain," replied Batman. "Now that you've remembered, the time stream will correct itself and you will transition back to our time."

Wonder Woman held up her hand. It was becoming transparent and glowing purple.

"It's happening already," said Batman. He handed back her lasso. "The Flash and I will get the others.

You make sure that Brainiac doesn't shrink the Earth."

As she became ever fainter, Wonder Woman opened her arms to her followers. "Steer clear of evil men such as Vandal Savage," she told them. "Remember that you are more powerful together than alone!"

Then Wonder Woman vanished to her own time.

Better get back to The Flash, thought Batman as he escaped the cave. *He must be bored out of his mind.*

CHAPTER 5: PIRATES!

THE FLASH WAS FAR FROM BORED. He was keeping up his pace on the Cosmic Treadmill while avoiding the snapping teeth of a pair of velociraptors.

Hidden from the dinosaurs behind the Batmobile, Batman pulled two spring-loaded nets out of the trunk, and tossed them at the velociraptors.

"Oh . . . look," gasped The Flash, "who's . . . back. . . ."

Batman hopped into the driver's seat, and set the digital clock. "There's no time to chat," he said. "Next stop, 1741. Step on it!"

The Batmobile rocketed off the cliff, and exploded above the jungle through a glowing rift in time.

The Treadmill zapped them above an ocean. The Batmobile splashed down in the waves.

"Whoa!" cried The Flash. "We're going to sink!"

Floatation devices popped out on either side of the Batmobile. "Relax," Batman said. "The Batmobile is prepared for virtually anything." His handheld device chirped. He spotted a pirate ship sailing toward them.

"Does it come with a Batman-Pirate costume?" asked The Flash. By the time he spoke, Batman was already wearing one.

Batman leaped onto a passing great white shark. He grabbed onto its fin, and rode the man-eating beast toward the pirate ship.

When he got close, Batman yanked the shark's fin, causing it to leap across the ship's deck. Batman waved at the stunned pirates as he passed overhead.

Batman dropped toward the deck, landing in a crouch in front of the captain.

"Well," the captain said, "ye be a long way from land there, matey."

"I lost me ship to a hungry kraken," replied Batman. "I had to commandeer that passing sea critter for travel. Call me Bat Beard."

The captain peered at Batman. "I see no beard."

"I shaved," Batman replied.

The captain nodded. "Any man that can tame a great white as fearlessly as ye is welcome on me vessel," he said. "Work hard and fight alongside us and ye will get part of the plunder. What say you?"

Batman scanned the pirates, but it took a second for him to recognize Green Lantern. Dressed in green rags, his teammate cowered in the corner, scrubbing the wooden deck. He had forgotten he was fearless. Batman had to make Green Lantern remember who he was.

"I say huzzah!" shouted Batman.

"Huzzah!" the pirate crew cheered.

The captain pointed at Green Lantern. "Now, ye yellow-bellied swabby, show him to his hammock."

Green Lantern led Batman below deck, to the crew's quarters.

As soon as they were alone, Batman gripped Green Lantern's shoulders. "It's me, Batman."

"Who?" Green Lantern replied nervously. "I thought you said you were Bat Beard. If the Captain knew you were lying, he'd . . . well, I don't know what he'd do but I'm afraid to find out."

"You aren't afraid of anything," Batman reminded him. "Your power ring, where is it?"

"The Captain took it when he fished me out of the sea as payment to be on his crew," Green Lantern answered. "It's locked up in his treasure chest."

"We have to get it," decided Batman. "It might be the only way to help you remember who you are."

"Are you mad?" gasped Green Lantern. "If the captain found out, he'd keelhaul us!"

"Fine, I'll do it myself," said Batman. "But I need a distraction. Will you at least do that for me?"

"Oh . . . okay," Green Lantern agreed.

Following Batman's plan, Green Lantern went up to scrub the deck across from the captain's cabin. He knocked over a barrel with his brush.

The barrel rolled, bashing into other barrels that tumbled everywhere. The original barrel smashed into a pirate, knocking him down. The captain hurried out of his cabin to find pirates running to avoid barrels.

"Ye clumsy oaf!" the captain hollered at Green Lantern. "You've befouled my ship, you lousy landlubber!"

As the crew gathered around to watch the captain yell, Batman sneaked behind them to the treasure chest. He opened the lid and picked up the power ring off a pile of gems.

"Find anything interesting?" the captain asked.

Batman spun around. The captain and the entire crew stood behind him.

"The number one rule of the sea, laddie," said the captain. "Keep your hands off the captain's booty."

"You ratted me out?" Batman asked Green Lantern.

"You did good, swabby," the captain assured Green Lantern. "It's time for our sticky-fingered friend to take a little walk . . . on the plank!"

The pirates grabbed Batman, and hauled him to the side of the ship.

Batman secretly tossed the power ring to Green Lantern.

Two pirates pushed out a plank over the churning ocean. The captain drew his sword and forced Batman backward on the walkway to nowhere.

"There is an old friend waiting to make your acquaintance," said the captain. He pointed at the great white shark circling below. Then he prodded the sword at Batman, forcing him closer to the end.

"Hal," called Batman, "I know that you are the most fearless man alive. Be that man."

"Stow yer scuttlebutt, matey," said the captain. "It's into the sea with ye!"

Batman teetered on the edge, with the shark snapping its giant teeth in the sea.

Green Lantern peered at his power ring uncertainly.

"I believe in you," Batman told him.

The captain started to laugh . . . but then stopped. "What in the blue blazes?" he gasped.

A tall green mast rose alongside the pirates' ship, followed by fluttering, glowing sails.

Green Lantern, in his super hero costume, floated in the air above the ship. His power ring blazed in his hand as his ship rose under Batman. "In brightest day," he chanted, "in blackest night, no evil shall escape my sight!"

He soared over to join Batman. "Let those who worship evil's might, beware my power—Green Lantern's light!

"I'm not your swabby anymore," said Green Lantern. He concentrated, and his ship blasted the pirate ship to pieces with glowing green cannonballs.

The pirates jumped off their sinking ship in terror.

Green Lantern noticed his body was becoming transparent. "Batman, I'm turning invisible."

"That's time repairing itself," Batman explained. "You're being sent back to our proper time."

As Green Lantern vanished into the future, his ship disappeared, too. Batman fell right into the driver's seat of the Batmobile.

The Flash was still running on the Cosmic Treadmill atop the vehicle. He looked exhausted.

The captain and the pirate crew popped up in the water beside the Batmobile.

Batman smiled at them. "If I were you, I would start swimming. My finny friend is nearby and I think he wants to say hello."

The captain and his crew swam away toward an island in the distance, the great white chomping at their feet.

Batman peered at The Flash. "You don't look so good." The Flash looked like he might collapse.

Batman opened his glove compartment, and pulled out a can with a bat-symbol on it. He threw it to The Flash. "This should help."

"You have your own vitamin drink?" asked The Flash.

"Crime never dries up," replied Batman, "but heroes can. That's why I developed my own vitamin supplement. Drink up, and let's go save Superman." He set the digital clock to the year 2116.

The Flash guzzled the beverage. "Whoa!" he cheered, his feet running faster until they blurred.

The Batmobile streaked across the ocean, spraying water along its sides, until it blinked out in an explosion of brilliant light.

CHAPTER 6: AN AWFUL FUTURE

THE FLASH PROPELLED the Batmobile into the future, where they landed in a broken-down, deserted Metropolis. Giant alien towers loomed over the rubble and abandoned cars.

"I thought the future would be flying cars," said The Flash, "or jetpacks, or robots—"

Two heavily-armed drones rose up in front of the Batmobile.

Both drones shot lasers at the Batmobile. Batman ducked in the driver's seat, but one laser hit the Cosmic Treadmill. Its runway snapped.

"Something's wrong!" The Flash cried.

"Hold on," said Batman. He hurled two explosive Batarangs at the drones, blowing them up.

The Batmobile shuddered and shook.

"We're losing temporal displacement energy," Batman explained. "Time is snapping the Batmobile to its proper place. Only one thing to do—" He leaped out of the sparking Batmobile.

"Batman!" The Flash shouted as the Batmobile began to fade out.

"Don't worry about me," called Batman. "Help the others!"

The Batmobile warped back into the past, leaving Batman alone on the ruined streets of Metropolis.

"Welcome to the future, Batman," said a familiar voice.

"Superman!" Batman called to the figure approaching in the shadows. "I've found you."

"Thank Brainiac," replied Superman. "Don't you just love the upgrades he gave me?

"You see, Brainiac from your era figured out you were traveling through time to rescue me, which meant future Brainiac also became aware of your plans. So he sent me to destroy you on arrival. It's so funny how this time travel stuff works, isn't it?"

Instead of waiting for a reply, Superman shot sizzling beams of heat vision at Batman.

Batman rolled behind an abandoned car, which bore the brunt of the blast.

"We hope you enjoy your time here in Brainiac-tropolis before you are vaporized," said Superman.

With a flip to the side, Batman spun and hurled Batarangs at Superman. They bounced off the robotic Man of Steel. Batman slipped down into a manhole and disappeared into the maze of the sewers.

Batman remembered something his friend The Flash had once suggested he do. *I bet Wayne Enterprises constructed a tunnel from Metropolis to Gotham City*, Batman thought. He searched the tunnels until he found exactly where he would have dug it himself.

With rocket-powered roller-skates strapped to his boots, Batman zoomed through the underground tunnel from Metropolis.

After hours of rolling, Batman paused to sniff the air. "Gotham City," he said. "I can smell it."

Using a flashlight, Batman found a secret branch that led to the Batcave. He flipped switches to get the electrical generators going. Lights flickered on.

Batman walked around his long-neglected hideout. The wreckage of vehicles, furniture, and keepsakes littered the floor. His giant penny was one of the few exhibits still standing upright.

He strode toward a large, rusty safe. *Behind this door lies the key to Earth's salvation*, he realized.

In a loud, crashing explosion of rock, Superman tunneled down through the roof of the cave.

"Oh, hey, Batman," said Superman cheerfully. "Boy, I'm a little disappointed to find you here. Fleeing to the Batcave? Kind of predictable, don't you think?"

CHAPTER 7: BATTLE IN THE BATCAVE

AS SUPERMAN LANDED on the rocky rubble, Batman scurried to hide in the shadows.

"You still resist me?" Superman called out. "None can stand up to the Brainiac Collective." He spotted movement in a corner of the cave, and zapped it with his heat vision.

It was only a fluttering bunch of bats.

"Come out, Batman," shouted Superman. "Don't you remember? I am the best at hide-and-go-seek. You can't hide from *me*."

"Don't you remember?" Batman yelled back. "You never played hide-and-go-seek with *me*."

A door in the cave wall swung open. Batman thumped out, wearing a gigantic armored suit studded with powerful weapons.

"Besides," Batman said, "who says I'm hiding?"

Superman floated in the middle of the Batcave. "So the Dark Knight dons his armor," he said. "It doesn't stand a chance against my super-strength." He charged over and swatted Batman.

Even in the heavy suit, Batman was flung across the cave. He clanged against the big safe with a pained grunt. Quickly, he climbed back to his robotic feet, and leaped at Superman, punching him into a wall.

Superman fought back, spinning Batman into the big penny, which collapsed on top of him.

Batman hoisted the penny off his armored back.

He grabbed a humongous statue of a Tyrannosaurus Rex, and bashed Superman with it, smacking the Man of Steel with dinosaur teeth.

But he couldn't damage the invulnerable Superman, who knocked Batman down.

Floating above Batman, Superman prepared to melt his armor with his heat vision.

At the last second, Batman rolled away. Superman's heat vision melted the safe behind Batman.

"Thank you," said Batman. "That safe was too rusted for me to open."

Inside the safe were two things: a glowing crystal of Kryptonite and some strange device.

"Your old Kryptonite stash," said Superman. "Hey, I finally turned evil and now you get to use it on me. When you plan ahead you really plan ahead!"

Batman grabbed the device, and attached it to the chest of his armor. "Kryptonite's not part of the plan today," he replied. "This is."

The bat-symbol on his armor blazed with dazzling light. A beam shined out and sizzled Superman.

Superman crumpled to the ground.

Batman pinned Superman down, zapping him again with the intense beam.

"What is—?" Superman groaned.

"Yellow sunlight," answered Batman. "Concentrated and magnified one thousand times. Enough to power up Superman . . . and melt down Brainiac."

Superman's robotic parts and circuits glowed red in the brilliant sunshine.

"No!" gasped Superman, struggling to get away. "You'll never—"

"Fight him, Superman," urged Batman. "I know you're still in there!"

Superman punched Batman in the center of his armored chest.

Batman was thrown across the cave, smacking into a wall, and collapsing on a ledge. The beam of sunlight winked out as his armor fell apart. Batman tried to get up, but he was too weak from the blow.

Superman flew over, and raised his foot, ready to stomp Batman. "Superman is no more," he said in a terrible robotic voice. "There is only Brainiac. Your friend is gone forever."

But Superman paused with his foot raised over Batman's body. "Friends," he murmured. He winced and shook his head. "Batman?"

"It's me, Superman," Batman said, pulling himself to his knees. "You can do this! You can fight this. Do it for Earth, do it for the Justice League!"

Superman struggled for control over Brainiac. He pulled at the mechanical parts of his body, spinning into a glowing whirlwind as he battled. Bursts of power sizzled around him.

Batman watched, his eyes narrowed, unsure who would win control, but hoping it would be his friend.

The whirlwind broke apart. Superman flew up, puffing out his chest, revealing that all the pieces of Brainiac's circuitry were gone.

He lowered himself down to Batman. "You did it," he said. "You saved me. You could have defeated me with your Kryptonite. But your sun ray device . . . how did you know it would wake me from Brainiac's influence?"

"I didn't," Batman replied. "But I had to take that chance. It's my job to prepare for the worst that this world can throw at me. But . . . I also always prepare to help a friend in need."

Superman clapped Batman on the shoulder. "Thank you, Bruce. Now let's go get Brainiac." But Superman suddenly started to glow and become transparent. "What's happening?"

"Now that you remember," explained Batman, "you're being drawn back to your own time."

"Why aren't you?" asked Superman.

"Unfortunately," replied Batman, "I'm stranded here."

"No!" Superman gasped, becoming more invisible.

"Make my sacrifice worthwhile," Batman told him. "Make sure you stop this future from ever happening."

Superman faded until he was almost entirely gone.

"Goodbye," said Batman, "my friend."

After Superman vanished back into the present, Batman stood for a long moment in the empty ruins of the Batcave.

But he had another surprise stashed in the vaults from the present.

CHAPTER 8: BOTTLED UP

SUPERMAN RETURNED to present-day Metropolis. There he found that his teammates in the Justice League, with some help from Supergirl, had beaten Brainiac's drones.

"Nice work, team!" he called.

"Wait a minute," said The Flash. "Where's Batman?"

Superman frowned. "Batman wants us to save the Earth from Brainiac. We'll have to figure out how to retrieve Batman from the future later."

Everyone on the Earth gasped or cried out as the sky suddenly changed to a sickly red. Up in space, Brainiac fired his shrink beam, and the planet dwindled until it was the size of a basketball.

The Justice League watched, horrified, as Brainiac's ship approached the now-tiny Earth.

Outside the atmosphere, Brainiac's ship extended metal pincers. They carefully plucked the Earth from orbit, and pulled the planet into Brainiac's spaceship. The Earth was lowered into a little glass specimen jar.

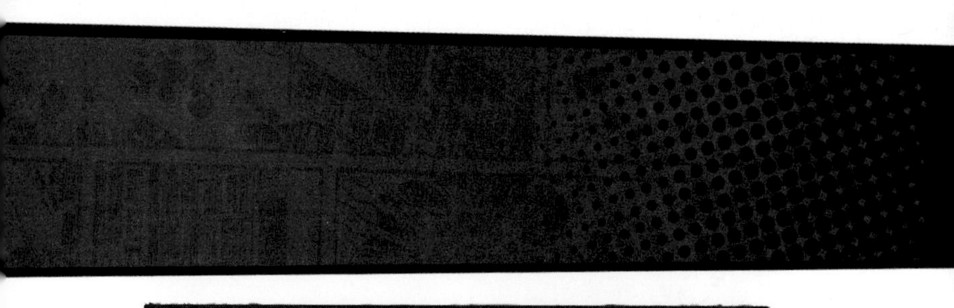

Everyone pointed up at a humongous cylinder being lowered toward the Earth.

"It's massive," said The Flash.

"It's scary," said Cyborg.

"No," said Wonder Woman, "it's . . . it's—"

"It's a bottle," said Batman.

All his teammates whirled around. Batman stepped out of a glowing blue sphere.

"You're back," breathed Wonder Woman.

Superman rushed over to his friend. "How did you get here?"

Batman tilted his head toward the glowing blue bubble beside him. "Time Sphere," he replied. "It was

just powerful enough to—"

Before he could finish, the Time Sphere cracked with jagged sparks of lightning. It fell apart in a heap.

"Let's get uncorked and un-shrunk," said Batman.

Cyborg rubbed his metal chin. "Even with our combined strength we're going to need more power to move that big cork," he said. He grinned. "I think I have just the thing."

Soon the members of the Justice League soared through the sky in awesome hi-tech jets Cyborg had customized for each of them.

"All right, team," Batman radioed the others. "Let's all concentrate our firepower in one area. Follow my lead."

The six jets zoomed upward in formation toward the vast cork stoppering the bottle holding the Earth.

"Wait for it . . ." warned Batman, urging them to hold their fire until they got closer to the cork. "Batarangs away!" he hollered.

All the heroes fired their jet weapons, which were amped-up versions of their own powers.

They all concentrated their fire on one edge of the cork, and their combined firepower began to push

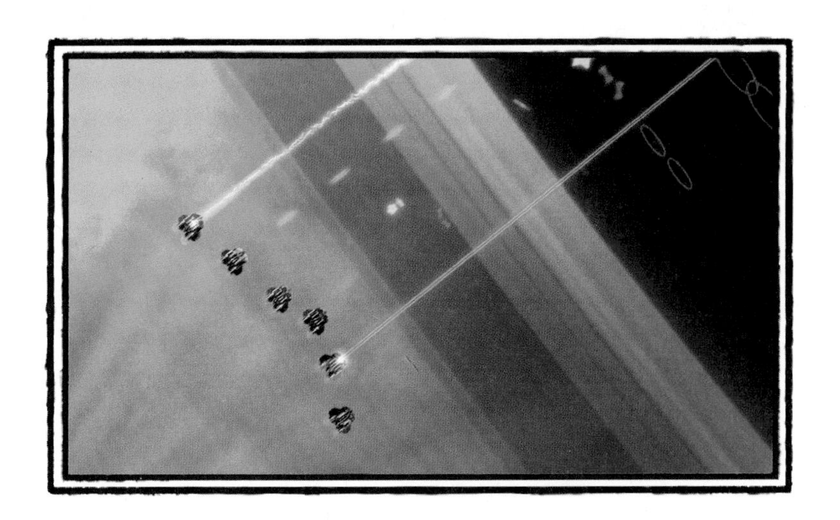

the stopper out of the bottle. The cork slowly inched upward, until it suddenly flew free with a loud *pop*! The stopper bounced off the table and rolled across the floor of the enemy spaceship. It spiraled to a stop at Brainiac's feet.

"Uncorked," gasped Brainiac. "One of my worlds is no longer in its original packaging." He stomped toward the bottles of his planetary collection.

The Justice League had already flown out of the bottle in their jets.

CHAPTER 9: BRAINIAC'S BRAIN

THE JUSTICE LEAGUE flew their jets in circles around Brainiac, buzzing him.

"A very clever escape," said Brainiac. "Let us see how clever you are once I zap you into nonexistence!" He blasted shrink-rays out of his eyes.

"Evasive maneuvers!" ordered Batman.

The Justice League's jets soared wildly, avoiding the shrink-rays.

Brainiac growled in pain and frustration as the Justice League dodged his attacks.

Superman's jet fell into formation beside Batman's. "We've got to figure out a way to turn off his ray."

"I might have an idea," said Batman, "but it means you have to keep him distracted."

Superman nodded. "Consider it done, Batman." As Batman's jet dived downward, Superman contacted the others. "All right team, let's do this."

They all buzzed their jets around Brainiac like a swarm of bees.

The Flash flipped on his turbo boost, and swirled around Brainiac so fast the robot got dizzy trying to spin and follow him.

While Brainiac was woozy, Wonder Woman rammed the robot's chin, punching him backward.

Using his frost breath cannon, Superman froze

Brainiac into an icicle, although ice only held the robot for a moment.

While Green Lantern fired green lasers, Cyborg shot Brainiac with his sonic cannon.

Brainiac was so disoriented that he didn't notice Batman zooming his jet toward his head.

"Engaging air brakes," said Batman. His jet stopped short, and Batman was ejected into the air. He soared toward Brainiac's head, and passed through a glowing portal in the giant robot's skull, slipping inside without Brainiac noticing.

After landing expertly, Batman scanned the alien technology inside Brainiac's head. While Brainiac battled his teammates outside, Batman made his way deeper into the

robot's brain. In the front, he found a crystal structure that shot the shrink-rays. out of Brainiac's eyes.

"The Justice League is giving me such a headache!" complained Brainiac as he swatted at the jets surrounding him.

Batman watched the war from the inside of Brainiac's head. "Fascinating," he said. He found the device creating the rays. It had two sides, one green and one red.

While Batman tinkered with the technology, Brainiac started gaining the upper hand outside. He smacked down the jets, and their weapons weren't doing any real damage. He was just too big for the Justice League to handle in their shrunk-down size.

"We're losing this thing," Green Lantern warned.

"I don't mean to be negative," The Flash added, "but we're doomed."

Brainiac slapped the side of his head, and Batman popped out one of the portals on the other side.

"Wrong, Flash," said Batman, as the Batplane swooped under him and caught him in its cockpit. "We've only just begun. Cyborg . . . execute Plan M."

CHAPTER 10: THE BIG LEAGUE

"IT'S TIME FOR OUR SECRET WEAPON," Cyborg said with a smile. "Initialize Mecha-Leaguer!"

All their jets fell into tight formation. Electricity arced between all their vessels. The jets pulled even closer together, morphing and combining their pieces as they linked up into a bigger whole.

"This does not compute!" Brainiac gasped as he watched the brilliant transformation.

"Okay, Brainiac," said Superman. "It's time to pick on someone your own size."

Brainiac peered down at Mecha-Leaguer, amused. "You would match your pathetic automaton against the most advanced robot in the universe? Fatal error."

To his surprise, Mecha-Leaguer punched Brainiac so hard that the robot was flung backward across the room.

"Thank my speed fist," said The Flash.

Brainiac leapt back up and rushed at Mecha-Leaguer. The two technological creatures smacked and slapped at each another.

"Come on, Cyborg, let's do our spinning kick," Superman suggested.

Mecha-Leaguer spun on one leg. Then he kicked out and slammed Brainiac with his boot. Brainiac toppled backward into his wall of jars.

"Forming green Sledgehammer of Justice!" Green Lantern hollered. He used his increased power ring abilities to create a giant weapon. Mecha-Leaguer leaped toward the downed Brainiac, and walloped him with the glowing sledgehammer.

Brainiac lay on the floor, frazzled and sparking.

"It's time to surrender, Brainiac," said Superman.

"Never!" shouted Brainiac defiantly. "I will shrink you out of existence!" The robot's eyes glowed, and they fired two bright beams at Mecha-Leaguer.

"Wonder Woman, now!" shouted Batman.

Wonder Woman raised Mecha-Leaguer's arm that was made out of her jet, blocking one beam like she would with a golden bracelet. The other beam hit Mecha-Leaguer in the chest, while the one Wonder Woman blocked hit the bottle holding the Earth.

Mecha-Leaguer and the Earth started to grow.

"That wasn't my shrink-ray!" cried Brainiac. "It was my growth ray! But how?"

"Easy," replied Batman. "While I was in your brain, I reconfigured the circuits of your shrink-ray device, reversing its polarity. So, instead of shrinking us . . . you *grew* us."

Batman held up a small device. "Before you think you can use either of them again . . ." he said as he pressed a button. A little explosion detonated in Brainiac's head, destroying the weapons. Smoke curled out of the portals on his skull.

"My rays!" shrieked Brainiac. "No!"

In seconds, the Earth grew so big that it burst Brainiac's spaceship into pieces.

Mecha-Leaguer and Brainiac were thrown free into space. Mecha-Leaguer righted himself and gathered all the bottled worlds from floating away as

Earth returned to its proper size and orbit.

"Recalculating!" gasped Brainiac desperately. "I am defeated. With my programming to collect stymied, this unit has no choice but to self-destruct, taking everything in this vicinity with it. Begin countdown. Ten . . . nine . . . eight . . ."

"Oh, man," said The Flash. "I thought we just won this thing."

"Hold on, Brainiac," said Batman. "You say that all you need to do is fulfill your programming to collect?"

Brainiac paused his countdown. "Affirmative."

"I think I have a solution," Batman said.

Back on Earth, Batman introduced Brainiac to the wonders of coin collecting . . . inside a prison cell.

"A Buffalo penny," cheered Brainiac. "This will be a perfect place to start." He placed the penny in an album. "Does anyone have more coins? I must collect them all."

The next day, the super heroes gathered in the Hall of Justice.

"So what happens when Brainiac collects all the coins?" asked The Flash.

"Impossible," Batman

replied. "They mint new coins every year, so his collection can never end."

"Ingenious!" Cyborg cheered.

Superman nodded at Batman. "Thank you for saving us. I'm sorry for saying that we were merely work friends."

Green Lantern stepped up beside Superman. "It's obvious by the way you were able to snap us out of our amnesia that you know a lot about us, as only a true friend would."

Wonder Woman smiled at Batman. "Thank you for being our friend."

"You're welcome," Batman replied. "Now I have something to say." He narrowed his eyes sternly. "This

team is in sore need of discipline. The next threat to Earth is going to find us prepared! Why? Because of this new training exercise I've devised called . . . Hide-and-Go-Seek!"

His teammates' mouths dropped open in surprise.

"Not *it*," said Batman. He dropped a smoke bomb and vanished.

"Not *it*!" Superman, Wonder Woman, The Flash, and Green Lantern echoed. They raced off to find hiding places, too.

"Wait," said Cyborg. "What?"

"Aw, man," sighed Cyborg. "I'm *it* again. Well . . . you know what? I'm starting the counting at fifty!"